MANGO
makes music

Bani McSpedden & Chris Gilvan-Cartwright

LITTLE HARE

This is Mango.

Mango loves noise!

But none of the other animals in the
jungle love noise as much as Mango does.

So Mango decides to say goodbye
to his friends and move to the big city.

He walks all night beneath the bright stars,
until at last he reaches…

...the noisy city!

He's amazed by the

roaring cars,

rumbling trucks,

rattling buses,

people talking, shouting,

rushing past.

Scraping,

squealing,

clattering,

clanging,

banging,

blaring.

There is so much noise...

...that Mango wants to run...

and run...

and run...

Then he sees a familiar shape. A tree!
He scurries up the trunk, disappears into
the branches and, exhausted, curls up to sleep.

Next morning, Mango is woken by a loud shout.

"Hey! You can't sleep there!"

"I've just come to the city, and I have nowhere to live," Mango explains.

"Well, if you'll help me out around the park," says Steve the park ranger, "you can stay."

Mango thinks this is great.

Working with Steve keeps him busy all day,

and building his new tree-house keeps him busy all night.

But sometimes, when everyone goes home and the
park is empty and quiet, Mango starts to miss his friends.
Tucked up in his tree-house, Mango feels a bit lonely.

One night, Mango hears a strange noise floating up from the street. He clambers down from his tree for a closer look.

He sees a small girl with huge hair, an amazing round face and amazing round eyes.

Mango thinks she looks

amazing!

She is holding a very curious object in her hands, and coming out of it is the noise Mango could hear from his tree-house.

The girl sees Mango and stops. "Hullo there," she says. "I'm Isobell. Isobell with two l's."

"What's that you're doing?" Mango asks.

"I'm playing my saxophone," Isobell replies.

"Do they all make that noise?" says Mango.

"It's not noise!" says Isobell. "It's music —

beautiful music."

"Do you think I could play it too?" Mango asks.

"Certainly not," says Isobell. "It takes years to learn how to play even one note."

"*Years?*" says Mango.

Then he has an idea.

The next morning, he is at the music shop trying out all sorts of things.

Things you blow…

and strum…

and pluck…

and squeeze.

It's hard work!

Hours later, Mango comes out of the shop
with a pile of oddly shaped parcels.
No one sees Mango for days.

At last he is ready. Mango waits till he hears the
sound of Isobell's saxophone in the late-night air,
then he joins in with his own noise.

Isobell looks around to see where the sound is coming from.
A group of people gathers.
And then they see a wondrous sight…

Up in the branches of Mango's tree are congas and bongos, beaters and bells, rattlers and shakers, cymbals and gongs — things of all shapes and sizes.

Mango's hands are a blur moving between them.
Isobell can't resist joining in.

Soon there's a whole crowd by the tree.
People are clapping their hands, tapping their feet,
and cheering Isobell and Mango on.

Steve is there, too, and he starts a conga line which threads
and spreads its way all through the park.

"This is so much fun! You can play with·me anytime,"
Isobell yells.

"It's amazing!" Mango calls back.

He knows he'll never have a lonely night again.

This book is dedicated to those who tap to a different beat.
With special thanks to Noni — Bani

For Isobel and Bluebell — Chris

Little Hare Books
45 Cooper Street, Surry Hills
NSW 2010 AUSTRALIA

National Library of Australia
Cataloguing-in-Publication entry
McSpedden, Bani.
Mango makes music.

For children aged 3-7.
ISBN 1 877003 08 5.

Monkeys – Juvenile fiction. I. Gilvan-Cartwright,
Christopher. II. Title.

A823.3

Designed by Kerry Klinner
Printed in Hong Kong

5 4 3 2 1